W9-BFZ-601

Trouble is brewing in the fish tank.

"Don't you ever, ever, ever feed the fish unless I let you," Russell told his sister. "They could die if they ate too much."

"I promise," said Elisa.

Later, Elisa tiptoed into Russell's room. She sat down next to the tank and watched the fish. She wished that she could give the fish something to eat. Tiny cookie crumbs would probably taste delicious to them, she thought. But she remembered her promise to Russell.

Elisa had gotten a large bottle of bubble bath liquid for her birthday. It worked like magic. You poured a little into the bathwater and the tub became filled with bubbles. Elisa wondered if maybe the fish wouldn't enjoy a bubble bath, too. . . .

"A good choice for reading aloud . . . and for [readers] ready for easy chapter books."

—*The Bulletin of the Center for Children's Books*

PUFFIN BOOKS IN THIS SERIES

"E" Is for Elisa
Elisa in the Middle
Make Room for Elisa
Rip-Roaring Russell
Russell and Elisa
Russell Rides Again
Russell Sprouts

Johanna Hurwitz

ELISA in the MIDDLE

illustrated by Lillian Hoban

PUFFIN BOOKS

PUFFIN BOOKS
Published by the Penguin Group
Penguin Putnam Inc., 375 Hudson Street, New York, New York 10014, U.S.A.
Penguin Books Ltd, 27 Wrights Lane, London W8 5TZ, England
Penguin Books Australia Ltd, Ringwood, Victoria, Australia
Penguin Books Canada Ltd, 10 Alcorn Avenue, Toronto, Ontario, Canada M4V 3B2
Penguin Books (N.Z.) Ltd, 182-190 Wairau Road, Auckland 10, New Zealand

Penguin Books Ltd, Registered Offices: Harmondsworth, Middlesex, England

First published in the United States of America
by William Morrow and Company, Inc., 1995
Reprinted by arrangement with William Morrow and Company, Inc.
Published in Puffin Books, 1998

7 9 10 8 6

LIBRARY OF CONGRESS CATALOGING-IN-PUBLICATION DATA
Hurwitz, Johanna.
Elisa in the middle / Johanna Hurwitz ; illustrated by Lillian Hoban.
p. cm.
Summary: Five-year-old Elisa has an older brother and a new baby brother, but her
elderly neighbor says the middle is the best, just like the filling in a sandwich.
ISBN 0-14-038783-8 (pbk.)
[1. Brothers and sisters—Fiction. 2. Babies—Fiction. 3. Family life—Fiction.
4. Schools—Fiction.] I. Hoban, Lillian, ill. II. Title.
[Pz7.H9574E1 1998]
[Fic]—dc21   97-34652 CIP AC

Printed in the United States of America

RL: 2.7

For Eileen and Eric Wilcock
Far away, but close in spirit

Contents

Russell's Little Sister
1

Russell's Fish
14

Marshall's Big Sister
27

Elisa's Chickens
41

Elisa's Glasses
57

Russell Writes a Book
73

Russell's
Little Sister

Late last spring Mrs. Michaels announced to her children, Russell and Elisa, that they were going to have a new baby in their family. Right away Russell, who was nine, said that he wanted a brother. "I already have a sister," he reminded his parents. "I don't need another one."

"Well, I want a sister," five-year-old Elisa insisted. "I already have a brother."

"We'll have to wait until October and see," Mrs. Michaels explained.

And so they waited and waited. While they waited, Elisa finished nursery school and began kindergarten. While they waited, Russell finished third grade and began fourth. And while they waited, they moved into a larger apartment in the very same building where they had always lived. Now Elisa and Russell each had their own room. And there was even a small room for the new baby. The new apartment was painted, and all of the Michaelses' furniture and clothing and pictures and books were transferred from their old apartment on the second floor to the new one. Now they lived on the fourth floor.

Finally, after all these other things had been accomplished and lots of time had passed, it was October, and the new baby was born. The baby turned out to be a brother named Marshall.

Russell was very pleased. At least he was as pleased as he could be about another person in their family who was noisy and smelly and somewhat of a nuisance. It was bad enough that he had a little sister to annoy him. Now there was a little brother, too. However, it would be a long time before baby Marshall would be big enough to reach the top of Russell's chest of drawers or the top shelves of the bookcase. So he knew his favorite models and his favorite books were safe. It was Elisa he had to worry about.

For a whole minute after she heard the news, Elisa was disappointed about the baby. She had so much looked forward to having a little sister. She knew she would have been such a good big sister to a little girl. She would have taught her so many things and played so many wonderful games with her. Then it occurred to Elisa that she could be a good big sister to a little brother as well. She liked the fact, too, that she was no longer the baby in their family. Now Russell would have someone else to tease instead of her. Elisa knew that she would never tease Marshall. She was going to be the best sister in the world to him.

"You're in the middle," Elisa's elderly neighbor Mrs. Wurmbrand told the little girl when she came to see the new baby. "You have a brother on each side of you, but the middle is the best," she whispered in Elisa's ear when Russell wasn't listening. "Just as the middle of a sandwich is the best part, too."

Elisa liked that. It was one of the surprises about having a big brother and a little brother. She was the sister in the middle, and Mrs. Wurmbrand said she was the best.

"I've got a surprise for you," Russell told Elisa.

"What is it?" she asked him eagerly. Elisa loved surprises.

Russell paused a moment so that Elisa would become impatient waiting to hear his announcement.

"What is it?" she asked again.

"The surprise is that there is no surprise," said Russell, grinning wickedly.

Tears welled up in Elisa's eyes, but she blinked them away. She was not going to give mean old

4

Russell the satisfaction of having made her cry.

"I don't care," said Elisa, walking away. "I didn't want a surprise anyway."

Elisa didn't understand why Russell teased her so much. She tried very hard to be a good sister to him. She was always ready to play with him when he didn't have a play date with one of his friends. She always let Russell choose the games. She tried to be helpful, too. The only problem was that her helping didn't always work out as she planned.

For example, back last spring, before Marshall was born and when they still lived in their old apartment, Russell had bronchitis. He was so sick that he missed a whole week of school. When he was better and returned to his class, he discovered that he had missed a lot of work.

"I need to catch up," he complained when he came home from his first day back. "Especially in my math workbook."

"I'm sure you'll be able to catch up in no time," said Mrs. Michaels.

"Ketchup?" asked Elisa. "How can he ketch-up?"

"He'll have to give up watching television for a few evenings and do more work," their mother explained.

"It's not fair," said Russell. "It's not my fault that I was coughing and had such a bad sore throat. First I was sick. And now I have to catch up on so much work."

"School can't stop just because you weren't feeling good," Mrs. Michaels said patiently.

Russell kept grumbling. "I don't feel like doing my math now," he complained.

"You can do it after supper," said Mrs. Michaels. "Let's go to the park now and get some fresh air. You can ride your bike," she suggested.

So they went to the park and Russell rode his two-wheeler and Elisa rode her tricycle. But all the time she was riding she was thinking about how she could help Russell. She, too, thought it wasn't fair. Last week he had spent almost all his time in bed sleeping or complaining. He had

6

missed going to the birthday party of one of his classmates, and his throat hurt him. He complained that his head ached, too. When Mrs. Michaels gave him the medicine that the doctor had prescribed, Russell made a face. He said it tasted yucky.

Now that he was all better, Russell should have been happy. Instead he was angry because he had to ketchup. Elisa didn't quite understand why he had to do it. But there were lots of things she didn't understand. And if Russell didn't want to do it, then, Elisa decided, she would help him. In fact, it would be a wonderful surprise for her brother.

When they returned home, Elisa waited for her chance. She hung around the kitchen, and when her mother left the room for a moment, Elisa quickly opened the refrigerator and removed the bottle of ketchup.

In their old apartment Russell and Elisa shared a bedroom. So Elisa slipped into their room, holding the bottle behind her. Russell was lying on the floor, reading a comic book.

"Don't bother me. I'm busy," he told Elisa.

Elisa didn't say a word. Quietly she hid the bottle behind her bed and played with Airmail, her rag doll. She whispered very softly into Airmail's yarn hair because the doll didn't have any ears. "I'm going to make a good surprise for Russell. He has to ketchup his math for school."

"Stop making so much noise," Russell complained. He was in a very bad mood.

Elisa stopped talking and kissed Airmail. Pretty soon the doll would be able to see what the surprise was.

Just then the telephone rang. Mrs. Michaels picked it up in the kitchen. A moment later she called to Russell. "The call is for you," she shouted. "It's Jeremy."

Russell sprang up at once and hurried to the kitchen. Jeremy was one of his best friends, and he had moved far away to New Jersey.

"Now!" Elisa whispered to Airmail. "I can do

it now." It wasn't necessary to whisper with Russell out of the room. But for some reason Elisa whispered to her doll as she worked. She opened her brother's backpack, which was lying on the floor. Even though she could only read the letters of the alphabet and a very few real words, Elisa was able to pick out the mathematics workbook. It was the one with all the numbers.

She didn't want to mess up Russell's bed or the floor. So she took the workbook over to the little table that was in the room. She turned the pages till she came to the first page that didn't have any of Russell's pencil marks on it. This must be the page where he had to ketchup, she decided. She went over to her bed and got the bottle she had hidden. It wasn't easy, but she managed to unscrew the bottle top. Then she turned the bottle upside down.

The problem with ketchup, she remembered, is that sometimes it pours out of the bottle too fast and other times it seems to stick inside and not want to come out at all. This was one of the times when the ketchup didn't want to come out. Elisa shook the bottle. Nothing happened. She shook the bottle again and again. A tiny trickle of ketchup began to slide down the inside of the bottle. This was hard work. No wonder Russell didn't want to ketchup his math. At this rate it would take a long, long time to ketchup all the pages in his book.

Mrs. Michaels walked into the bedroom. "Elisa?" she asked in surprise. "What in the world are you doing?" She grabbed the glass bottle out of Elisa's hands just as the first tiny dribble of red sauce landed on the page.

"I need it," Elisa protested. "I'm helping Russell ketchup his math."

"Oh, my goodness," shouted Mrs. Michaels. She began to laugh.

"What's so funny?" asked Elisa. "I can do it. It's a surprise for Russell."

"It's a surprise all right," gasped Mrs. Michaels, still laughing. She began to wipe the tears from her eyes. "Hurry. Bring me a tissue.

We have to clean up Russell's workbook at once."

"Why can't I help him?" asked Elisa, puzzled and disappointed.

"Russell has to *catch up* with the rest of his class," said Mrs. Michaels, trying to pronounce the words as clearly as she could so her daughter would understand the difference between *catch up* and *ketchup*.

Unfortunately Russell returned to the room in time to see the blob of ketchup on one of his homework problems. He didn't think it was funny at all.

"Elisa was just trying to help you," said Mrs. Michaels, defending her daughter and laughing at the same time.

"The best help would be no help," he said. "The best help would be for her to leave this room."

Elisa's eyes filled with tears. She didn't want Russell to be angry at her. She had only wanted to be a good sister and help him.

Luckily it was suppertime. It should have

been a good distraction from Elisa's mischief and Russell's annoyance. Unluckily they were having hamburgers, and so the ketchup bottle came to the kitchen table with everyone and everything else.

Russell's Fish

Now that they lived in the new apartment, Elisa and Russell each had their own room. At first Elisa wasn't sure that she liked having her own room. It was scary at night to be alone in the dark without her big brother nearby. Each night she clung to Airmail and waited for something bad to happen.

"What could happen to you?" asked Mr. Michaels.

"I don't know," Elisa admitted.

"Maybe she's afraid of ghosts," said Russell smugly.

"Don't be absurd," said his father. "There's no such thing as a ghost. Elisa knows that."

"Maybe she's afraid of monsters," said Russell. "There are no monsters in my bedroom. But maybe there are monsters in her room."

Elisa hadn't even thought about ghosts and monsters. Now she was even more afraid of being alone in her room.

"I want to sleep in Russell's bedroom," she said.

"There's only one bed in my room. You can't sleep there," Russell pointed out. "Besides, it's my own special room. It's not your room."

"Elisa, honey," said Mr. Michaels, giving his daughter a hug, "don't listen to Russell. He's just teasing. We wouldn't have rented an apartment with ghosts or monsters in it. And besides, there

15

is no such thing as a ghost or a monster. You could look all over New York City and you would never be able to find one. So tonight, when you go to bed, you just close your eyes and go to sleep. Mommy and I are in the room down the hallway, and Russell is across the hallway, and soon our new baby will be sleeping across the hallway, too. Everyone will be safe. I promise you."

Elisa listened to her father's words. It was easy to believe him during the daytime. When the sun was shining, Elisa wasn't afraid of anything. In fact, when it was daytime, she was glad she had her own room.

It was fun to play in her room with Airmail and the other dolls. She could make tea parties with her little dishes or line up the chairs and play school. Russell wasn't there to tease her and make fun of her games. If she left Airmail sitting on a chair, she knew she could leave the room and Airmail would remain on that same chair. In the past there had been a strong possibility that she would return to find Airmail standing on her head. It was even worse when Airmail was missing. Russell liked to play hide-and-seek with the doll. He'd hide her somewhere in the house when his sister wasn't looking. Sometimes it had taken ages and ages until Elisa could find Airmail again.

In the night, when she was bathed and in her pajamas, Elisa lay in bed, clutching Airmail. Her grandmother had made matching pajamas for the doll. "Don't be afraid," Elisa whispered. "There's no such thing as ghosts."

Elisa listened hard. Was there something in her room? She thought she heard a sound.

The next thing she knew, Elisa heard the sound of her mother pulling up the window blinds. "Good morning," said Mrs. Michaels, smiling at her daughter. The sun was shining in through the window. Somehow the night had come and gone and nothing bad had happened. Elisa kicked off her cover and jumped happily out of bed.

After a week or so Elisa and Airmail fell asleep

without thinking anymore about scary things.

"I knew you'd like your own room," Mrs. Michaels told her daughter. "Everyone needs a little privacy in their life."

Russell especially loved his privacy. He liked to work on making models of planes and ships without having his little sister breathing down his neck. Sometimes the work was very delicate, and if she accidentally jiggled his arm, he would drop the very small piece he was trying to attach. He liked to be able to read by himself, too. He had become a supergood reader, one of the best in his class. But reading was no fun if Elisa was pestering him to read out loud to her when he wanted to read quietly to himself.

When Marshall was born, their grandmother came for a visit. She brought Russell a wonderful gift. It was a small aquarium with four brightly colored striped fish swimming in the water. There was also a dark brown snail that seemed stuck to the side of the glass tank. But if you left the room and returned later, the snail seemed to have mysteriously unstuck itself and moved to another location.

"He's cleaning the tank," Russell explained to Elisa.

Elisa nodded her head and pretended that she understood. How could a snail clean the tank? It didn't have any soap, and it didn't have a sponge.

At the bottom of the tank there were colored pebbles and a couple of larger rocks. The fish swam around and around in the tank. Once a day Russell would feed them some grains of food from a little box. The fish swam quickly up to the top of the water to retrieve the tiny morsels of food.

One day, as a very special treat, Russell permitted Elisa to feed the fish. Her fingers smelled funny afterward from the food.

"Don't you ever, ever, ever feed the fish unless I let you," Russell told his sister. "They could die if they ate too much."

"Okay," Elisa agreed, nodding her head.

"Remember. You must never, never, *never*

feed the fish unless I let you and I'm watching you," Russell said again.

"I promise," said Elisa. She certainly wouldn't want to harm her brother's pet fish.

Elisa liked looking at the fish, but she felt sorry for them. They got such a little bit to eat, and the food didn't look the least bit delicious. Furthermore, she thought it must be boring for the fish to swim around and around and around all day in such a small space.

One rainy afternoon, when Russell was off visiting one of his friends and Marshall was sleeping, Elisa tiptoed into Russell's room. She sat down next to the tank and watched the fish. It didn't matter to fish if it was a rainy day or a sunny day, she thought. Even sunny days were wet for them inside their aquarium tank.

Elisa wished that she could give the fish something to eat. Tiny cookie crumbs would probably taste delicious to them, she thought. But she remembered her promise to Russell. She would not feed the fish any cookie crumbs or even any of their own smelly fish food. But she wished there were something she could do for them.

She watched them swim from side to side in their tank. Back and forth, back and forth. It didn't look like fun to her at all. When she was in the bathtub at night, sometimes she pretended she was a fish, too. But she didn't have to do the same thing night after night. She had many bath toys that she could play with, and sometimes she took a bubble bath. Bubble baths were loads of fun.

Elisa had gotten a large bottle of bubble bath liquid for her birthday. It worked like magic. You poured a little into the bathwater and the tub became filled with bubbles. Elisa wondered if maybe the fish wouldn't enjoy a bubble bath, too.

Elisa tiptoed to the bathroom. She pushed the stool that she stood on when she brushed her teeth up close to the bathroom sink. Above the sink was the medicine cabinet, and inside the cabinet was the bottle of bubble bath. Mrs. Michaels was resting in her bedroom, and Elisa was so quiet that her mother didn't hear a thing.

Elisa took the bubble bath and tiptoed back to Russell's room. She smiled to herself, thinking how happy the fish were going to be. She opened the bottle and poured some of the liquid into the fish tank. Then she put her hand into the cold water in the tank and swished the bubble liquid around. Soon there were lots of bubbles in the fish tank. The fish swam around the bubbles and through the bubbles. Elisa knew they were having a lot more fun than before.

She watched for a few minutes more and then went back to her own room. She could hardly wait for her mother to wake from her nap. Then she would show her what a good time the fish were having.

But that wasn't what happened at all. Half an hour later, when Mrs. Michaels woke, Elisa took her mother into Russell's room.

"I want to show you something!" she announced with great excitement.

"What is it?" asked Mrs. Michaels, puzzled.

"Look at the fish!" Elisa exclaimed. She ex-

pected to see them swimming happily around in the bubbles. Instead the fish were doing a new trick. They were floating at the top of the tank. They had never done that before.

"What happened to them?" asked Mrs. Michaels, looking at the fish through the bubbles. "Elisa, did you feed them?" she asked suspiciously.

"No, no," said Elisa. "I wouldn't feed them. I promised Russell I would never do it unless he let me."

"What did you do?" asked Mrs. Michaels.

"I gave them a bubble bath," said Elisa. "I thought they would have a good time, like I do at night."

"Elisa. You didn't," said her mother, horrified.

"Yes, I did," said Elisa.

"Elisa, you've killed Russell's fish. Fish can't live in soapy water. They are not little girls."

"I killed them?" asked Elisa. She could hardly believe the news. She began to cry.

"All right. All right," said her mother soothingly. "I know you didn't mean to do it. But you have to learn that you can't just do things without thinking of the consequences."

"I didn't know," Elisa said, sobbing.

"That's true, you didn't. And I certainly never thought of telling you," her mother admitted. "Come. Blow your nose. We'll phone Daddy at work and see if he can stop at the pet shop on his way home and bring some new fish for Russell. But you must promise never to put anything into the fish tank. Not even your finger. And if you get a good idea, check it out with me first."

So that was why Russell got four new fish and a new snail before the day was out.

Unfortunately for Elisa he got home before the new fish arrived. Of course, he was furious at her.

"You never told me that fish don't like bubble baths," she said to him.

"You never told me that little sisters could be this awful," he complained to his mother. "There *is* a monster in Elisa's bedroom. It's *her*," he said angrily.

Mrs. Michaels made Elisa apologize to her

brother and promise it would never happen again.

"Never. Ever," said Elisa solemnly.

And it didn't. But of course, that didn't mean that Elisa didn't do other things: some good, some bad. That's the way little sisters are.

Marshall's Big Sister

"Elisa is my big helper," Mrs. Michaels always told everyone when she went walking with her daughter and the new baby.

Elisa smiled proudly. She loved to take Marshall for walks. She helped her mother push the carriage, and she talked to Marshall all the time.

"That's a water hydrant," she said, pointing out

the sights along the street. "Some people say 'fire hydrant,' but that's silly. Only water comes out of it."

Marshall was lying flat on his back, looking up at the sky, and didn't seem to care what it was that Elisa was talking about. By the time they walked only one block, Marshall had fallen asleep.

"The baby is one month old," Mrs. Michaels told one of her neighbors who stopped them along the street to admire the infant.

"Marshall is one month *young*, not one month old," Elisa corrected her mother. It was amazing how many mistakes people made when they were talking.

Yesterday Elisa had gone with her mother and Marshall for his one-month checkup from the pediatrician. "We're taking a bus," Elisa had informed the baby in her mother's arms. "But that really means that the bus is *taking us*."

Even though he couldn't answer her, Elisa liked talking to Marshall. It was a little like talking to her doll Airmail. Neither said anything, but still she talked away. Whenever she learned a new song at school, she was certain to sing it to both of them. It was too bad that Airmail would never learn to speak, but one of these days Marshall would be able to sing along with her.

"The wheels on the bus go round and round..." and "The eentsy-weentsy spider..." and "There was a farmer had a dog." Elisa could hardly wait until Marshall could join her in spelling out all the letters B-I-N-G-O. It would be loads of fun.

In the meantime, of course, Marshall just looked around. He kicked his feet, he waved his hands, and he cried. When Marshall cried, it made Elisa feel sad. Sometimes it made her feel like crying, too. She would go into her bedroom and put her hands over her ears.

"Crying is the only way that Marshall can talk to us now," Mrs. Michaels explained to her daughter.

"It's the way he tells us that he is hungry or wet or restless," Elisa's father pointed out.

"It's awful," Russell complained. "How can I practice my violin when Marshall makes so much noise?"

"Once upon a time you used to cry, too," Mr. Michaels told Russell.

"Did I cry, too?" asked Elisa.

"Of course. All babies cry. But Russell was the champion crier. He could cry longer and harder than any other baby I ever knew," said their mother.

"I don't believe it," said Russell. He went into his bedroom and closed the door behind him. Soon they could hear the sound of his violin playing.

Although Elisa wanted to hold her baby brother, Mrs. Michaels was afraid that he was too heavy for her. Instead she put Marshall in Elisa's lap when Elisa was sitting on the sofa. Elisa beamed with pride. She liked the soft, cuddly feel of her little brother. She liked the way he smelled after he had his bath.

Sometimes Elisa wanted to give Marshall one of her toys to play with. But when she put a bright red crayon into one of his tiny hands, her mother took it away.

"Marshall can't play with crayons or small

things that he can put into his mouth," she told Elisa.

That made Elisa feel sad. She wanted to share her toys with Marshall like a good big sister.

When Elisa baked cookies at her friend Annie's house one Saturday afternoon, she brought home one cookie for each member of her family.

"This is delicious," said Mr. Michaels, complimenting his daughter's baking skill. "But you can't give one to Marshall. He is too young to eat cookies with raisins. He could choke on a raisin."

"I'll eat Marshall's cookie," Russell said eagerly.

Elisa was disappointed. She had carefully counted out enough cookies at Annie's house so everyone in her family could eat one.

"You could eat the extra cookie yourself," suggested her mother. "You worked hard to bake it. Now you can eat it."

"Thanks a lot," said Russell with disgust. He had been hoping to get the extra cookie.

"I'll share it with you," said Elisa. She broke

the cookie in half and gave a piece to her older brother.

"You took the bigger piece," Russell complained.

But Elisa had already put the whole piece of cookie inside her mouth, so there was really no way to check it out.

"Don't be so greedy," Mr. Michaels said to Russell.

Marshall just smiled and kicked his feet. He didn't even mind that he was too little to eat cookies.

On Halloween, when Elisa came home from trick-or-treating, she showed Marshall all the goodies she had collected. "I'll trade you," said Russell when he saw what Elisa had in her bag. "You can have this box of raisins for that chocolate bar."

"No," said Elisa. She had her own box of raisins.

"I'll give you the box of raisins and a lollipop for the chocolate bar," said Russell.

"No." Elisa had three lollipops in her loot bag. "I'll trade you the chocolate bar for your raisins, three lollipops, and the package of chewing gum," she offered.

"Forget it," said Russell. He went into his room with his bag of treats.

"I'd give you my chocolate bar, and you wouldn't even have to trade anything," Elisa told Marshall. It was an easy offer to make. She knew that Marshall couldn't accept it. Still, she really thought she meant it.

One evening Marshall was crying and crying in his crib. He couldn't have been hungry because he had just eaten. He didn't need to be burped because Mrs. Michaels had patted him on the back many times. He didn't need a clean diaper because he had just been changed.

"It's too soon for him to be teething," Mrs. Michaels told her husband.

"What's teething?" asked Elisa.

"Teething means growing a new tooth, and it hurts the baby's gums," her mother explained.

33

"So babies always cry when they are teething."

Elisa had recently lost her first tooth, and a new one was already poking through the gum to fill the empty space.

"I don't cry when I'm growing new teeth," she said proudly.

"That's true," said Mrs. Michaels. "But when you were a baby Marshall's age, you cried a lot. All babies do."

Elisa wished she could do something to help Marshall. She watched as her mother walked back and forth, holding the baby. Marshall's face was red and angry looking. The sound of his crying filled the whole apartment.

Elisa buried her face in Airmail's soft body. She didn't want to look at Marshall when he was crying and so red.

For a second Marshall stopped his noise.

"Look," said Mrs. Michaels. "He's reaching for Airmail."

Sure enough, the rag doll that was Elisa's favorite toy had distracted Marshall.

"Let's see if he'll stop crying if we put Airmail in his crib with him. Maybe he'll even go to sleep," said Mrs. Michaels.

Although Elisa had wanted to share her toys and her cookies and candies with Marshall, she wasn't sure if she wanted to share Airmail. Airmail was very special to her.

Marshall waved his arms and made some grunting noises.

"He's trying to tell us that he likes Airmail, too." Mrs. Michaels laughed. "Why don't you let him have your doll for a few minutes? He can't break her," Mrs. Michaels added.

Elisa kissed Airmail good-bye. Then, reluctantly, she surrendered her doll. "He can have her while I take my bath," she said. "But I need her when I go to sleep."

"Of course," said Mrs. Michaels.

Her mother laid Marshall down in his crib and Elisa put Airmail beside him. Then she waited to see what would happen. Marshall touched the doll and poked gently at it.

Mrs. Michaels went into the bathroom and adjusted the faucets so the water was just the right temperature for Elisa's bath. In the tub Elisa played with some little plastic boats. The boats sailed gently through her bathwater until she splashed hard enough to sink them. Then they bobbed up to the top of the water again. While she was playing in the water, she didn't think about Airmail. But as soon as she was out of the bath and dried and in her pajamas, she went to claim her doll.

Marshall had fallen asleep on top of Airmail. Elisa went to get her mother to help her retrieve her rag doll.

"How about leaving Airmail where she is for now?" whispered Mrs. Michaels. "In a little while, when Marshall moves in his sleep, I will bring her to you."

"I want Airmail now," Elisa insisted.

"Let's have a little talk," whispered Mrs. Michaels. She took Elisa out of Marshall's room and into Elisa's own sunshine yellow room. "Now we don't have to whisper," she said.

"I want Airmail now," Elisa said again.

"If I take Airmail out from under Marshall, he may wake up and begin crying some more. Wouldn't it be nice if he slept quietly for a while? I promise you that Airmail will be in your bed when you wake up in the morning."

"It isn't fair." Elisa pouted. "You said I'd get Airmail back when I finished my bath."

"I know I did," agreed Mrs. Michaels.

"Marshall couldn't have any of the other things I tried to give him. How come he can have Airmail when I don't even want him to have her?"

"Wait a minute," said Mrs. Michaels. She went to the linen closet and returned with two boxes. "Here are two gifts that Marshall received when he was born," she said.

Elisa watched as her mother opened the boxes. In one box there was a white teddy bear. In the second box there was a toy monkey that looked as if it were made from oversized socks. The monkey had a long tail and a funny hat sewed on its head.

"I didn't realize that Marshall was ready for

these stuffed toys. Now I see that he is. How would you like to have one of these animals in your bed for now? In the middle of the nigh⁺ I'll switch the monkey or the bear for Airmail. Marshall doesn't love Airmail the way you do. He just needs something cuddly in his crib."

The sewed-on hat was very silly, and the monkey had a big smile on its face. Elisa looked at it. She looked at the white teddy bear, too.

"I'll take the monkey," she said. "But you really, really promise me that when I wake up, Airmail will be here?"

"I promise," her mother said, tucking her into her bed. "Marshall is very, very lucky to have you for a big sister. You are letting him borrow your favorite toy. He is too little to understand that, but I do. And I know it proves what a wonderful, generous big sister you are."

Elisa smiled at her mother and squeezed the monkey closer to her. When her mother turned off the light, the monkey's softness felt almost as comforting as Airmail. And when Elisa woke in the morning, the monkey was gone, and there was Airmail in her usual place. It was just as Mrs. Michaels had promised.

"I am the best sister in the world," Elisa told Airmail. "And you are the best doll."

Elisa's Chickens

Every morning Elisa blew Marshall a good-bye kiss before she went to school. She was proud to be in kindergarten this year. She loved it. Kindergarten was much more fun than nursery school, and it lasted all day long. Now Elisa had a lunch box, just like Russell did. And every morning her mother put a sandwich, a container of juice, and a cookie inside. Sometimes there was a small bunch of grapes or some apple slices wrapped in plastic as well. After the first few days of learning new names and new rules, Elisa felt right at home. She loved Ms. Cassedy, who once long ago had been Russell's kindergarten teacher, too. Maybe someday, when Marshall grew to be old enough, Ms. Cassedy would be his kindergarten teacher also.

It was funny to think of Marshall in kindergarten. Now he was so little and soft and helpless. It didn't seem possible that someday he would grow as big as Elisa.

Besides the fun of making lots of new friends and the thrill of eating lunch at school, Elisa loved all the new things that she was learning. She had a reading readiness workbook. Since she already knew the whole alphabet, she felt very ready to read, and Ms. Cassedy complimented her frequently because she never got her letters confused the way some of the other boys and girls did.

Elisa learned many new songs and new games. She especially looked forward to the time each day when all the children sat on the floor with their legs crisscross applesauce and Ms. Cassedy read aloud to them. Elisa loved listening to the stories. She could hardly wait until she knew how to read all by herself, just like Russell. Almost every day she came home from kindergarten with a new piece of information that she had learned. Soon she would be every bit as smart as Russell. So there.

Right away at the beginning of the school year the kindergarten class studied the seasons. School began in the autumn. Some people said "autumn," and some people said "fall," but they were both the same.

"In the autumn the leaves fall down," Ms. Cassedy pointed out to her students.

Elisa raised her hand the way she had been taught. "Yesterday I falled down in the park and hurt myself," she told her teacher. She pulled up her skirt to show the new scab that was forming on her knee.

"You *fell* down," said Ms. Cassedy sympathetically. "I'm glad you're better now."

43

"I fell, too," called out one of the boys in the class.

"Me too," called out someone else.

"I fell hundreds of times," said still another voice.

"Shh," said Ms. Cassedy, raising her hand and making the V with her fingers that was a signal for attention.

Gradually all of the children raised their hands in the V signal, too, and the room was quiet.

Ms. Cassedy lowered her hand, and they all lowered theirs, too.

"Raise your hands if you ever fell," she instructed her students.

All the boys and girls raised their hands.

"Hands down," said Ms. Cassedy. "Everyone falls sometime," she told the kindergarten class. "And leaves fall off the trees in the autumn season. But they don't fall off every tree." Then she showed the children pictures of evergreen trees—trees that would stay green forever and not lose their leaves in the autumn.

"Later we will take a walk in the park and see

if we can find any evergreen trees," Ms. Cassedy told her students.

Whatever Ms. Cassedy told her students, Elisa came home and told her family. "I knew that already," Russell would say each time Elisa reported some new piece of information.

"That's very interesting," Mrs. Michaels would say.

"You sure are learning a lot at school these days," Elisa's father would say.

Of course, Marshall still couldn't say anything at all. Nevertheless, Elisa talked to him all the time and shared her new information with him.

"The more you talk to Marshall, the more he'll learn to understand your words. Before you know it, he'll be talking back to you," said Mrs. Michaels to Elisa. Mrs. Michaels was busy changing her baby son's diaper. Elisa was standing nearby, holding her nose and watching. She was always curious about the baby. Someday she would be a mother, too. She wondered how she would ever manage to hold her nose and change a diaper at the same time.

One day Elisa came home from school with a load of new information. "We were talking about birds and chickens," she told her family at supper. "Did you know that they grow out of eggs? The mother bird makes the eggs and sits on them to keep them warm. Then the baby birds hatch out of the eggs."

"Everyone knows that," said Russell, cutting into his baked potato.

"Chickens come out of eggs, too," said Elisa, ignoring Russell.

"That's very interesting," said Mrs. Michaels.

"You sure are learning a lot of new things at school," said Mr. Michaels, smiling at his daughter.

"What I can't understand," said Elisa, "is how come there are no chickens inside the eggs we eat."

"That's because they are inside the refrigerator, where eggs are so cold they can't hatch," Russell explained.

After supper Elisa took her bath. While she was splashing in the tub, she still thought about the eggs. Wouldn't it be wonderful if she could hatch an egg into a baby chick? she thought. As she washed, she hatched a little plan.

When bath time was over and Elisa had put on her pajamas and brushed her teeth, she went into the kitchen. The light was off, and no one else was in the room. Her mother was giving Marshall his evening bottle, her father was watching a news program on television, and Russell was in his bedroom doing his homework.

Elisa walked over to the refrigerator and opened the door. The little light inside showed her the row of eggs lined up on the shelf inside the door. Elisa counted one-two-three-four-five-six-seven brown eggs. Quickly she took two of the cold eggs, one in each hand, and let the refrigerator door slam shut by itself.

It will be a surprise for everyone, Elisa thought. She wouldn't tell anyone. Not even Marshall. She didn't have to tiptoe to her room because she was wearing her soft bedroom slippers. In the dark bedroom she laid the eggs gently on her bed, and then she turned on the light.

She wished she could sit on the eggs herself and warm them until they hatched. But she knew that she was too big to do that. If she sat on the eggs herself, they would be sure to break. She was glad that she had thought of that. Her mother would be proud of her for remembering that actions have consequences.

She opened the bottom drawer of her chest and made a little nest out of her short-sleeved summer T-shirts. She put a couple of shirts on top of the eggs to keep them as warm as a mother chicken would.

Of course, Airmail saw what Elisa had done. But no one else in the family did. First thing the next morning, before she went to the bathroom or took off her pajamas, Elisa opened the drawer to check on the eggs. They had not hatched into little chicks yet, but she was glad to feel that the eggs were no longer so cold. That was a very good sign.

In the kitchen Elisa heard her mother mumbling as she fixed breakfast. "I was sure I had more eggs than this," Mrs. Michaels said as she

cracked eggs into a bowl and began to beat them.

However, since Mrs. Michaels didn't ask if anyone had taken two eggs from the refrigerator, Elisa didn't think she had to say anything. Besides, she knew it would be a wonderful surprise for her mother when she had two baby chickens to show her. It would be fun to surprise Russell, too. He always seemed to know everything. He could do so many things. He could make such great models. But he had never made real live chicks. He had never thought of it. So there.

When she came home from school that afternoon, Elisa ran into her bedroom to check the eggs. There were still no little chickens in her drawer. Elisa wondered how long it would take for the eggs to be warm enough to hatch.

As she thought about it, her eyes spotted the metal radiator against the wall that kept her room warm. She went over and put her hand on it. Sure enough, there was heat coming up right now. If she put the eggs under the radiator, they could be warmer than in the drawer. Elisa wished she had thought about that last night. Too bad she had wasted all this time when the eggs could have been getting ready to hatch.

She took the eggs and a T-shirt from her drawer and remade the little nest. She slid the nest with the eggs under the back of the radiator. The nest didn't show, so no one would know it was there except her. She'd have to start thinking up good names for her little chicks, she thought.

After supper that evening and before breakfast the next day, Elisa got down on the floor and checked again for her chickens. Nothing had happened yet. Then it was the weekend. Elisa went to a birthday party on Saturday, and her father took Russell and her to the aquarium on Sunday. The new week began, and now Elisa's class was studying about the first Thanksgiving. They were going to cook a real dinner in their classroom. There was so much to think about that Elisa forgot all about the two brown eggs under her radiator.

One day, when she came home from school, she went into her bedroom, and there was a terrible smell. It was worse than Marshall's diaper smell. It was the worst smell that Elisa's nose had ever smelled.

"I don't know what it is," said Mrs. Michaels. "I noticed it just after you went to school this morning. I was vacuuming in your room, and suddenly there was this overwhelming odor. I opened the window, but it hasn't done much good. Whatever it is, the smell won't go away. I've phoned Mr. Harvey and left a message on his machine."

Mr. Harvey was the building's super. It was his job to fix things that were broken. During the summer, when Elisa had accidentally gotten locked in the bathroom, he had come and rescued her by removing the door.

Now Elisa held her nose and rescued Airmail. She grabbed her rag doll by the arm and ran out of the room with her. She hoped Mr. Harvey would come soon and fix her room. There was no way that she would sleep in a room with such a bad smell as that.

Elisa went to check on Marshall. He was

awake and kicking his little legs. Though he was still very small, he wasn't as red as he had been when he was born. She held Airmail up so she could see the baby. Then she put the doll under one of her arms and put her other arm between the bars of the crib. When her hand reached Marshall, she tickled his little feet. Then she put her finger into his little hand, and he clutched it tightly.

"He sure loves you," said Mrs. Michaels.

"Maybe I could sleep in here with him tonight," Elisa suggested. She would rather sleep on the floor in Marshall's room than spend the night with the bad smell in her room.

The doorbell rang. "I hope that's Mr. Harvey," Mrs. Michaels said to Elisa.

A moment later Elisa heard her mother and Mr. Harvey talking together.

"I can't begin to imagine what that stench is," Mrs. Michaels said.

Elisa waited with Marshall. She wondered if Russell had been right. Maybe the smell in her bedroom came from a monster.

A minute passed, and then another. Suddenly Elisa heard her mother calling her.

"I'll be right back," she told Marshall. She ran to her room. The smell was as strong as ever.

"Elisa Michaels. What do you know about this?" asked her mother in an angry voice.

Elisa looked where her mother was pointing. From under the radiator Mr. Harvey had pulled out her T-shirt nest. Neither egg had turned into a chicken. One of the eggs had broken.

Elisa had forgotten all about the nest. She was so surprised that she took her hand away from her nose to explain. "I was hatching chickens for us," she said. "Like we learned at school."

"So you put two eggs under the radiator," said Mrs. Michaels. "And I had the misfortune to break one when I was vacuuming this morning."

"They say boys are a handful," said Mr. Harvey, scooping up the foul-smelling T-shirt and the eggs. "But I think you better keep an eye on this young lady. She can get into more trouble than any number of boys I ever knew."

He went to the bathroom to flush the eggs away.

"I was trying to make baby chicks," said Elisa, crying. Even though she had forgotten about the eggs for a while, she remembered now how happy she had been at the possibility.

"Are you a hen or a little girl?" asked her mother.

"A little girl," said Elisa, sobbing.

"So of course you couldn't make chickens. Only mother hens can do that. And the type of eggs I buy at the supermarket would never, never hatch. They are special eating eggs."

"Oh," said Elisa. "I didn't know that."

"Well, now you do," said her mother.

"What do you want to do with this?" asked Mr. Harvey, returning to the room with Elisa's smelly T-shirt.

"Throw it in the garbage," said Mrs. Michaels. "Thank you so much for helping solve this mystery."

"It could have been worse," said Elisa.

"How could it have been worse?" asked her mother.

"You could have broken both eggs when you were cleaning."

"Or Elisa could have been twins," said Mr. Harvey.

Elisa's Glasses

When Mr. Michaels wrote a letter or brushed his teeth, he always did it using his right hand. When Mrs. Michaels beat some eggs or sewed on a button, she always did it using her right hand. When Elisa made a painting or ate her breakfast, she used her right hand, too.

Marshall was too little to use either of his hands very much. The most he did was wave them in the air. So no one knew whether he would be a right-handed or a left-handed person when he grew older. But Russell was left-handed.

He wrote his homework, brushed his teeth, fed his fish, made his models, and ate his meals using his left hand. That's just the way he was.

"My brother is left-handed, too," Mrs. Michaels would say to people, referring to Russell and Elisa's uncle Peter, who lived in California.

Russell felt very special being the only left-handed person living in their apartment. "Did you know that all famous and important people are left-handed?" he asked Elisa.

"Really?" she asked. She didn't know anything about it.

"Yes," said Russell. "George Washington and Abraham Lincoln were both left-handed."

Elisa was impressed.

"Christopher Columbus was left-handed," said Russell. He tried to think of the names of other famous people. "Dr. Seuss, Mr. Rogers, Santa Claus, and a lot of others, too."

"How do you know they are all left-handed?" Elisa wanted to know.

"I just do. And you know what else I know?" Russell asked his sister.

"What?"

"It means that someday I will be famous and important. But you won't," Russell told her. "Because you are not left-handed."

Elisa had never thought about becoming famous. Five-year-old girls were not usually famous. But maybe when she grew up, she would want to become important. Now she wouldn't be able to. It just didn't seem fair.

For the next few days Elisa tried hard to use her left hand instead of her right one. However, although she usually made good paintings, the pictures she did with her left hand looked awful. Furthermore, when she used her left hand, it was very hard to write in her reading readiness workbook. Her letters were all shaky and took up too much space. They looked as if a baby had written them. Worst of all, it took too long to make the letters with her left hand. So at school Elisa continued to use her right hand. Russell wasn't there to see her, anyhow.

At home Elisa brushed her teeth with her left hand. She tried to eat with her left hand, too. Sandwiches and glasses of milk were easy. Corn and peas were much harder. Hardest of all was trying to eat her morning bowl of cornflakes using her left hand. She just couldn't seem to control her spoon and get it to do what she wanted it to. She dribbled milk and cereal all over her clothes. So whenever possible, Elisa requested toast instead of cereal for breakfast. Toast was easy to eat with her left hand, but it was very hard to spread anything on it. Sometimes Elisa could get her mother to put the cream cheese or the jam on her toast for her.

One morning, as Elisa was trying to eat her cereal with her left hand, she noticed the newspaper that her father had left on the table. There were pictures of three important men and one important woman on the front page of the paper. Elisa guessed that all of them must be left-handed. Otherwise, according to what Russell had said, they wouldn't be able to become famous enough to have their pictures in the newspaper. She took another spoonful of her cereal. Her hand wobbled a bit as it made its way to her mouth.

Elisa looked again at the four people on the front page. She noticed something that she hadn't seen before. All of them were wearing eyeglasses. Elisa put her spoon down and touched the frames of her eyeglasses. Maybe Russell was wrong. Maybe you didn't need to be left-handed to be important. You needed eyeglasses.

A big smile spread across Elisa's face. She had eyeglasses, and Russell didn't.

Elisa picked up her spoon with her right hand and quickly and easily finished her breakfast. She didn't spill any of her cereal.

The next time Russell bragged to her about being left-handed, she laughed at him. "You're wrong," she told him. "Famous people wear eye-glasses. So there."

"Anyone can go get eyeglasses," said Russell.

But afterward Elisa noticed her big brother checking in the newspaper and the magazines that their parents subscribed to. Every time Russell saw someone without glasses, he brought the picture to show Elisa.

"I bet that lady does wear glasses," she told him when he showed her one such photograph. "She just took them off when she was having her picture taken."

During the day Elisa hardly ever took her glasses off. Colors were brighter and pictures and letters were clearer when she wore them. In fact, most of the time these days she even forgot she was wearing them.

In the evening after supper, when Elisa got ready for her bath, was the time she removed them. Nobody wore eyeglasses in the bathtub!

One Saturday morning, when Elisa woke up, she couldn't find her glasses. They weren't on top of her chest of drawers, where she usually put them. They weren't under her bed, where she occasionally put them. And they weren't in the bathroom, where she might have put them when she took them off.

"They can't be far," said Mrs. Michaels when Elisa told her that the glasses were lost. "You didn't leave them at school. You were wearing them when we ate supper. They must be somewhere in the apartment."

"Russell? Did you hide them?" asked Mr. Michaels sternly. Russell was known to tease his sister by hiding her things.

"No," said Russell.

"Are you sure?"

"Yes. Cross my heart. I wouldn't hide them," he said.

"Then it's up to you to find them," Mr. Michaels said to his daughter. "You have to be careful of them. Eyeglasses are not toys, you know."

"I'll look for them after breakfast," Elisa said. She was too hungry to look for them before she ate.

"Marshall is still sleeping," said Mrs. Michaels,

smiling. "He had a lot to drink while you were still asleep. So he'll probably sleep for another hour. How would you like me to make French toast this morning?"

"Yummy!" said Elisa instead of saying, "Yes."

"Great!" said Russell.

As soon as breakfast was over, Mrs. Michaels reminded Elisa to search for her glasses. Elisa looked again in her bedroom. They weren't there. Then she looked once more in the bathroom. They weren't there.

The doorbell rang while she was looking. It was Nora Resnick, their upstairs neighbor. Nora was twelve years old and very busy these days. Elisa hardly ever saw her anymore, so she ran to give her friend a hug.

"My mother would like to borrow some brown sugar if you have any," Nora told Mrs. Michaels. "We're going to make cookies this morning, but we're missing one of the main ingredients."

"Let me look," said Mrs. Michaels.

"Nora can help me look for my glasses while you look for the sugar," said Elisa.

"Are they lost?" asked Nora.

"She always loses things," said Russell.

"No, I don't," said Elisa.

"Yes, you do," said Russell.

"Where have you looked for them?" asked Nora.

"I looked all over my room. And in the bathroom, too."

"I think you have to look everywhere in this apartment," said Nora. "I know what. We'll each look in a different room." She turned to Russell. "You look in the living room," she instructed. "I'll look in Elisa's room. We'll ask your mother to look in the kitchen, and your father should search in your parents' bedroom."

"Where should I look?" asked Elisa.

"You check again in the bathroom," said Nora.

Because Nora was older than he was, Russell didn't protest. He went to the living room and began looking around. Elisa went into the bathroom and looked. The bathtub stood on clawed feet. She got down on her knees and felt around

66

underneath. She pulled out a plastic sailboat that she hadn't played with in many weeks. That was a nice surprise. She did not, however, find her glasses under the tub. The glasses were not on the sink or on top of the toilet tank. They were not inside the laundry hamper, either. There was no place else to look in the bathroom.

Elisa heard the doorbell ringing as she left the bathroom.

"Who is it?" she called through the closed door.

"It's Teddy," the voice on the other side answered. "I'm looking for Nora."

Elisa opened the door and let Teddy inside. He was Nora's *little* brother even though he was ten years old and bigger than Russell. "We're going to make cookies to take when we visit our cousins this afternoon. But we need brown sugar. And now we lost Nora. I thought she came here to borrow some from you."

"She is here," Elisa informed Teddy. "But she's helping look for my eyeglasses. I lost them."

"I'll help, too," Teddy offered.

"We're each looking in a different room," said Elisa. "You can look in Russell's room."

Teddy went off to search for the glasses. Elisa tried to think of another place to look. It seemed silly for her to be looking for her glasses without wearing her glasses. If she were wearing the glasses, she would see better and be able to find them. But if she were wearing her glasses, she wouldn't have to look for them because they wouldn't be lost.

Elisa heard Marshall beginning to cry in his bedroom. When he woke, he always gave one or two small cries and waited. Then, if no one came to him, he would begin to cry louder. Too bad Marshall wasn't older. Then he could help hunt for her glasses, too.

Elisa went into Marshall's bedroom. He was lying on his back, looking up at the mobile over his crib and kicking his feet. Elisa held her nose. He needed his diaper changed. Marshall's blanket was kicked to the foot of the crib. He wore special baby pajamas with feet so he didn't really need the blanket very much.

"Morning, Marshie," Elisa cooed to her brother in a nasal voice. Holding her nose made her voice sound different.

Elisa poked her hand through the bars of the crib. She put a finger into Marshall's hand.

Marshall kicked his feet and smiled at Elisa. He made some baby sounds.

"Mommy's coming to feed you in a minute," she told him. "She's busy looking for my glasses. They're lost."

She took her hand from her nose for a moment and tried to pull Marshall's cover up over him. There was something poking out from under the cover. It was red, just like the frames of her glasses. In fact, it was her glasses!

"Mommy, Mommy," Elisa called as she ran out of the room, looking for her mother. "I found them. I found my glasses."

Both of Elisa's parents and Russell and Nora and Teddy all came out of the different rooms of the apartment. "Look," called Elisa proudly. "I found my glasses."

"Where were they?" asked Nora.

"They were in Marshall's crib," she announced.

"What in the world were they doing there?" asked her mother.

"I must have taken them off when I was saying good night to Marshall last night, on my way to taking my bath."

"Then Marshall found them," said Nora.

"We both found them. Marshall and me," said Elisa.

"Russell, I found this book on the shelf in your room. Can I borrow it?" asked Teddy, holding up a book that he had discovered.

"Sure," said Russell.

"Nora, I found the brown sugar. It was behind the cornstarch and the box of oatmeal," said Mrs. Michaels.

"I found two nickels and a penny under the sofa cushion," said Russell. "Can I keep them?" he asked his parents.

"I found my old toy sailboat under the bathtub," said Elisa. "I'm going to play with it tonight."

"I found one of my cuff links," said Mr. Michaels. "It was under our bed. I didn't even know it was lost."

In the midst of everyone showing one another what they had found, the telephone rang, and Marshall began crying loudly. Mrs. Michaels went to pick up the baby. And Mr. Michaels went to answer the phone.

A minute later he returned. "That was your mother," he said to Nora and Teddy. "She wanted to know if I had seen her lost children. I told her you were here and would be going right back with the sugar that she wanted."

"I'm glad you found your glasses," Nora told Elisa as she and her brother left to return to their own apartment.

"Me too," said Elisa. "It was like a game. Maybe we can play it again tomorrow."

"Maybe not," said Mr. Michaels, giving Elisa a hug. "In fact," he said, laughing, "I'd say *abso-*

lutely not. You've got to learn to take better care of your glasses. Remember?"

"Okay," said Elisa. "I'll take care of them. And I'll think up a different game for tomorrow."

Russell Writes a Book

Last fall the elementary school that Russell and Elisa attended started something brand-new. It turned an empty classroom into a publishing center. The room was filled with computers and other equipment that could be used for making books. All the students in third, fourth, and fifth grades were busy these days writing their own stories. They had writing folders in their classrooms. In them they recorded the tales that they wrote. Then the stories were typed into the computers. Russell and his classmates were learning how to edit and correct their writing. After the stories were complete, the best one written by each child would be bound into a cover. It was very exciting.

The younger children in the school talked about books and listened to books that their teachers read aloud. They all were learning how to read books, and they could borrow books from the school library. But at least for the present the publishing center was only for the upper grades in the school.

Of course, it bothered Elisa that once again Russell was going to do something that she couldn't.

"It's not fair," she complained.

"You'll have your chance to write a book in a few years," promised Mrs. Michaels.

"I wish I could write a book right now," said Elisa.

"Writing is hard work," Russell complained.

He liked using the school computers. But he couldn't always think of something to write about.

"You could write about the time you got a new bicycle," his mother suggested the first time Russell complained that he didn't know what to write.

"That's boring," said Russell. Instead he wrote a story about a war among the dinosaurs. There was lots of blood and killing in his story. Seven dinosaurs were killed. Russell thought it was a good story. But it was a lot like the stories written by several other students in his class. It was amazing how many dinosaur wars took place in Russell's class.

"You have quite an imagination!" the teacher wrote on his paper. "Let's see if you can find another topic next time."

"You could write about moving from one apartment to another," suggested his father when Russell complained once again that he didn't know what to write about.

"That's boring," said Russell. Instead he wrote a story about Martians fighting people on earth.

They had super ray guns to zap one another. A hundred people got zapped.

"It's a science fiction story," Russell explained to his teacher. "I've been to the planetarium many times, and I know all about outer space."

"I hope they don't have any super ray guns in outer space," his teacher said. She helped Russell go over his spelling. "Perhaps in your next story you'll write about something more true to life," she suggested to him.

One day in March Russell came home from school all excited. There was going to be a competition for the best book written by an elementary school student. "It's not just for the best book in fourth grade. It's not just for the best book written by someone in our school. It's a contest for the best book written by any child in the whole city."

"Oh," said Elisa. She was very impressed. "Russell's going to be in a contest," she told Marshall.

The baby smiled at her. These days he smiled more and more. He still couldn't say anything. He still didn't have any teeth or much hair. But he was growing. And he could sit up all by himself.

"I don't know what to write about," Russell complained as usual.

"You could write about Marshall," said Elisa.

"He's boring," said Russell. "I can't write a book about him. He doesn't do anything."

"You could write about being in the Scouts," suggested his mother. "You do loads of things in the Scouts."

"That's boring," said Russell.

"Boring?" asked Elisa, surprised. "I thought you loved being a Boy Scout."

"Of course, I like being in my Scout troop," said Russell. "But that doesn't mean I want to write about it."

"You could write about playing the violin," said Elisa. Russell had been taking lessons for almost two years, and he was getting better and better at making music.

"A violin is not something to write about. It's something to play," said Russell.

"Well, I'm sure you'll think of something,"

Mrs. Michaels told Russell. "Maybe a good idea will just pop into your head."

"Like 'Pop Goes the Weasel!' " said Elisa. She began to sing the words to the song. Russell covered his ears and walked out of the room.

He went and did his math homework. He practiced the violin. He read his library book for his book report.

"Did anything pop into your head yet?" Elisa asked Russell when they were having supper.

"No," said Russell. He was glad Elisa didn't start singing again.

Russell watched a program on TV. He took a bath and shampooed his hair.

"Did anything pop into your head yet?" Elisa asked him.

"No," said Russell with irritation. "Leave me alone."

"How can I leave you alone?" asked Elisa. "I'm your sister."

Just then an idea popped into Russell's head.

Russell didn't talk anymore about his book.

"It's a secret," he said to his mother the next time she asked him about his writing project.

"It's a secret," he told Elisa when she nagged him about his book.

Elisa loved secrets. "I won't tell a single person. I promise," she said.

"I can't tell you. Then it won't be a secret anymore," said Russell.

At first Elisa tried to figure out what Russell's book was about. But because Russell didn't talk about it, after a few days she stopped thinking about her brother's story and the contest.

There were so many other things for her to think about instead. Every morning she peeked in Marshall's mouth to see if his first tooth had arrived yet. In the mail she received a package from her grandmother. It was a new outfit for Airmail. Grandma had made Airmail a pair of bright green slacks with an elastic waist. There was a little green and blue and yellow shirt for the doll to wear with the slacks. The blouse had four buttons.

Elisa was invited to parties three Saturdays in a row. All her school friends were turning six years old, and as a result, Elisa wore her party dress and ate a lot of birthday cake. She played party games and got several prizes. But even winning the first prize for pinning the tail on the donkey at Annie's birthday party didn't remind Elisa of the contest that Russell had entered. She had forgotten all about his book and the prize he hoped to win.

The April weather was beautiful. Every day after school Mrs. Michaels took Elisa and Marshall to the park. On the days when he didn't have violin lessons or Scout meetings or play dates with a friend, Russell came along, too. It was wonderful for Elisa to run around in the park without having to wear her heavy winter jacket. Without her jacket she felt light enough to fly. She went on the swings and the slide and climbed on the monkey bars. Sometimes she and her friends chased the fat pigeons that were walking about in the play area in search of something to eat. The pigeons flew off into the air. But a moment later they landed back on the ground. They seemed to know it was just a game, and they weren't afraid of the children.

One afternoon in May, when he didn't have a Scout meeting or a violin lesson or anything else to delay his coming straight home from school, Russell arrived home with big, big news.

"I won. I won," he shouted.

"You won?" asked his mother, looking puzzled.

"Remember the contest for the best book?" he asked her.

"You won that contest?" asked Mrs. Michaels excitedly.

"Yes. Yes. Yes. I entered, and I'm a winner. I won second prize!" shouted Russell.

"Second prize?" screeched Elisa, jumping up and down. "That's wonderful!"

"I'm going to get a plaque to hang up on the wall and a certificate so I can buy fifty dollars' worth of books at a bookstore."

"Fifty dollars! Russell, you're rich!" shouted

Elisa. She had never heard such good news before.

"Russell, I'm so proud of you," said his mother, giving him a hug. "Your father will be very proud of you, too."

"I dedicated the book to you and Dad," said Russell.

"I'm proud of you, too," said Elisa, although she wished that Russell's book had been dedicated to her. "And so is Marshall."

"There's going to be an award ceremony," said Russell, "and all the winners will attend. I'm the only winner from my whole school. My teacher said that a picture of all the winners will probably be in the newspaper."

"In the newspaper?" gasped Elisa. "That's wonderful."

Russell stood grinning at his triumph.

Suddenly Elisa thought of something. "Russell, if your picture is in the newspaper, then you'll be famous."

"That's right," said Russell proudly.

"So that means you were right," Elisa said. "You were right about left-handed people being famous."

"That's true," said Russell, nodding in agreement. He thought for a moment. "But I wouldn't have won the writing contest if I didn't have something good to write about."

"What did you write about?" asked his mother.

"I wrote about Elisa and all the crazy things she does all the time. Things like giving the fish a bubble bath or putting ketchup on my homework."

"You wrote about *me*?" Elisa asked with amazement.

Russell nodded. "The name of my book is *My Sister, Elisa*," he announced.

"You wrote about *me*," Elisa said again. "Then I'm going to be famous, too, even if I'm not left-handed."

"That's right," Russell said. "Besides," he added somewhat sheepishly, "I was only teasing you. I made it up about George Washington and Abraham Lincoln. I'm not sure if they were left-handed or right-handed."

"What about Santa Claus? And Dr. Seuss?"

"I don't know," said Russell, shrugging his shoulders. "Maybe they are left-handed. But I'm not sure about it."

Any other day Elisa would have been very angry to discover that Russell had been teasing her once again. But today she was too excited about being in his book to get annoyed at him.

Marshall was sitting in his high chair. He wasn't impressed with all this information about right hands and left hands and books and prizes. He let out a howl.

"He's still working on his tooth," said Mrs. Michaels, picking up the baby and rocking him in her arms.

"Maybe he's sad because he's not famous like Russell and me," said Elisa. She ran over and squeezed her little brother's hand. "Don't cry, Marshie," she said, stroking his soft arm. "When

I'm bigger, I'll write a book about you. Then all of us will be famous and important. Russell and me and you, too."

Marshall stopped crying. He looked at his big sister, and he made an enormous smile. If you looked hard, you could just see the tiniest bit of his first little tooth peeking through the gum.

Johanna Hurwitz has been a children's librarian with the New York Public Library as well as a teacher of college courses in children's literature. She is also the author of several books about Russell's neighbors, Teddy and Nora: *Busybody Nora, Nora and Mrs. Mind-Your-Own-Business, New Neighbors for Nora,* and *Superduper Teddy.* Ms. Hurwitz lives in Great Neck, New York.

Lillian Hoban was born and raised in Philadelphia, where she studied at the School of Industrial Art. She is the illustrator of the beloved books about Frances the badger and Arthur the chimpanzee, as well as numerous picture books. Lillian Hoban lives in Connecticut and New York.